Rafi and Rosi

Lulu Delacre

Children's Book Press, *an imprint of* Lee & Low Books Inc.
New York

Para Arturo
con todo mi cariño

Children's Books Press, an imprint of LEE & LOW BOOKS Inc.,
95 Madison Avenue, New York, NY 10016, leeandlow.com
Originally published by HarperCollins Children's Books

Cover design by Maria Mercado and Christy Hale
Book production by The Kids at Our House
The text is set in Times Regular
Manufactured in China by Imago
Printed on paper from responsible sources
10 9 8 7 6 5
First Children's Book Press edition, 2016
Library of Congress Cataloging-in-Publication Data
Names: Delacre, Lulu, author illustrator.
Title: Rafi and Rosi / Lulu Delacre.
Description: First Children's Book Press edition. I New York : Children's
Book Press, an imprint of Lee & Low Books Inc., 2016. I Series: Dive into
reading I Originally published by Rayo in 2004. I Summary: "Two tree frogs,
mischievous Rafi and his younger sister Rosi, learn about the plants and
animals of Puerto Rico together. Includes additional factual information and
activities about the topics covered in the story"— Provided by publisher.
Identifiers: LCCN 2015049760 I ISBN 9780892393770 (paperback)
Subjects: I CYAC: Tree frogs—Fiction. I Frogs—Fiction. I Brothers and
sisters—Fiction. I Natural history—Puerto Rico—Fiction. I Puerto Rico—Fiction.
Classification: LCC PZ7.D3696 Raf 2016 I DDC [E]—dc23
LC record available at http://lccn.loc.gov/2015049760

Contents

Glossary

ahorita (ah-oh-REE-tah): A Puerto Rican way of saying "later."

algae: Plantlike living things that lack true roots, stems, and leaves. They live in the water and can range in size from microscopic to 30 feet long or more.

¡Ay, bendito! (EYE, ben-DEE-toh): Oh, blessed!; Oh, dear!

¡Ay, caramba! (EYE, kah-RAHM-bah): Oh, goodness gracious!; used to express an emotion, such as pain, disappointment, or anger.

¡Chévere! (CHEH-veh-reh): Great!

cobito (coh-BEE-toh): A small hermit crab.

coquí (coh-KEE): A tiny tree frog found in Puerto Rico that is named after its song.

mangrove: A tropical tree that grows in swampy ground along the shore.

Parguera Bay: A body of water on the shores of the fishing village La Parguera in the town of Lajas. Lajas is on the southern coast of the island of Puerto Rico.

piragua (pi-RAH-gwah): In Puerto Rico, a snow cone flavored with fruit syrup, such as coconut, raspberry, or tamarind.

sí (SEE): Yes.

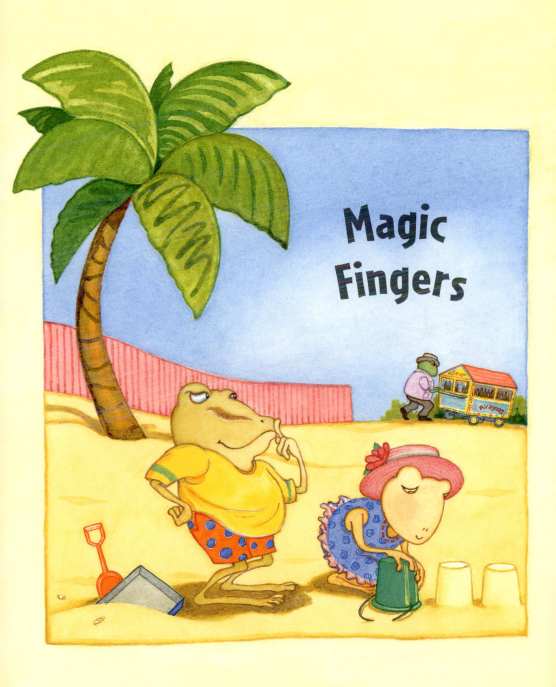

Magic Fingers

"A trick for a nickel!"

hollered Rafi Coquí.

"A trick for a nickel."

Rosi looked at her big brother.

"What are you doing?" she asked.

"I have magic fingers," said Rafi.

"I can turn gray sand

into white sand and black sand."

"Show me!" begged Rosi.

Rafi poured a shovel full of gray sand
onto a shoebox lid.
He took the lid with one hand
and placed his other hand under it.
He slowly moved the hand
under the lid back and forth.
Rosi watched how the black sand
moved away from the white sand.
Now there were two small piles.

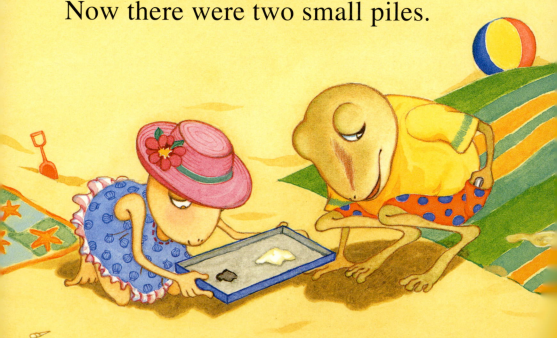

"Wow!" shouted Rosi.

"How did you do that?"

"I told you," said Rafi.

"I have magic fingers."

"Can I have magic fingers too?"
Rosi asked.

"Later," said Rafi.

"First, get me some customers
so we can buy a *piragua*."

"A trick for a nickel!"

hollered Rosi.

"A trick for a nickel!"

Other froggies gathered around.

"My brother has magic fingers!"

said Rosi proudly.

"Show them, Rafi."

Under the shoebox lid,

Rafi moved his hand back and forth.

Again he made gray sand

turn black and white.

"Great trick!" everyone said.

Nickels dropped

into Rosi's beach hat.

Then Pepe came over.

He was a bully.

"That's not magic," he protested.

"Oh, yes it is!" said Rosi.

"He truly has magic fingers!
Watch!"

13

Rafi did his trick,

but not fast enough.

In one quick movement

Pepe took the shoebox lid

away from Rafi.

"*¡Ay, caramba!*" Rafi yelled.

"I knew it!" Pepe shouted.

A thick magnet lay in the sand.

Rosi picked it up.

It was covered with black specs.

"What's this?" she asked.

"Ha!" Pepe said.

"A magnet covered with iron dust."

He stepped back and walked away.

"A magnet?" asked Rosi.

"So, where's the magic?"

Rosi began to cry.

Rafi looked at his magnet.

Then he looked at his little sister.

He hadn't meant to make her sad.

He took out a small red rag

and dusted off his magic tool.

"It still is a kind of magic,"

he said.

"How?" asked Rosi.

Rafi told her all about

how the magnet attracted

metals like iron.

It separated the black iron specks

from the true white sand.

"Yes . . ." agreed Rosi.

"It is a kind of magic. . . .

Can I have magic fingers now?"

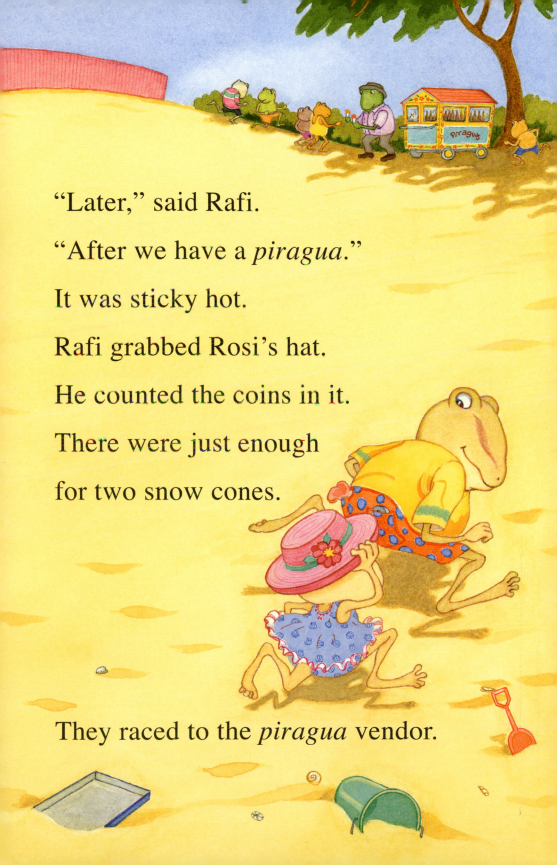

"Later," said Rafi.

"After we have a *piragua*."

It was sticky hot.

Rafi grabbed Rosi's hat.

He counted the coins in it.

There were just enough

for two snow cones.

They raced to the *piragua* vendor.

Rafi bought two coconut *piraguas*.

They were cold and sweet.

After they had licked
the paper cones clean,
Rafi took out his magnet.

"Here," Rafi told Rosi.

"Now I'll show you

how to have magic fingers too."

And he did.

"I did it!" yelled Rafi.

"I hit a mango

with my new bow and arrow."

Rafi looked at his sister.

Rosi was stringing

tiny red flowers.

She was humming a song.

"Do you want that big mango

up there?" Rafi asked Rosi.

"I'm sure I can get it for you."

Rosi kept humming.

"ROSI!" he shouted.

Rosi finished the crown of flowers
she was making
and gently placed it on her head.
Then she skipped along
to pick more flowers.

The sun was about to set.

Rafi and Rosi were going

to camp outside

by the famous Parguera Bay.

This was Rosi's first visit

to the bay of the glittering water.

On cloudy nights

many visitors came by.

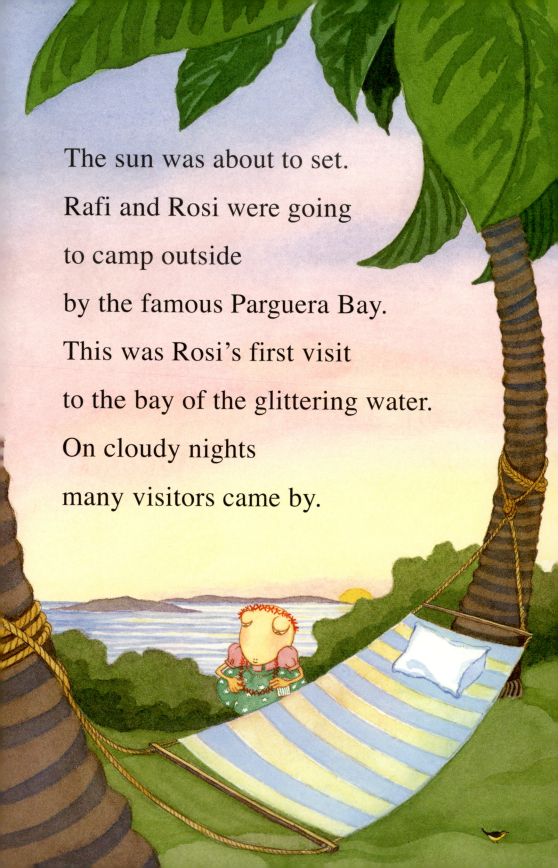

Rafi shot his arrow

at a tree next to the bay.

When he plucked the arrow

out of the trunk

he noticed how dark

the water had gotten.

He stirred its surface.

It was beginning to sparkle.

"Hmm . . . This gives me an idea,"

he said to himself.

Rafi turned to Rosi and said,

"I'm such a good shot!

I bet tonight I can shoot to the sky

and make all the stars come down."

Rosi stopped humming.

She looked at her brother.

"You can't do that," she said.

"*Sí, sí*, I can," Rafi replied.

"You'll see."

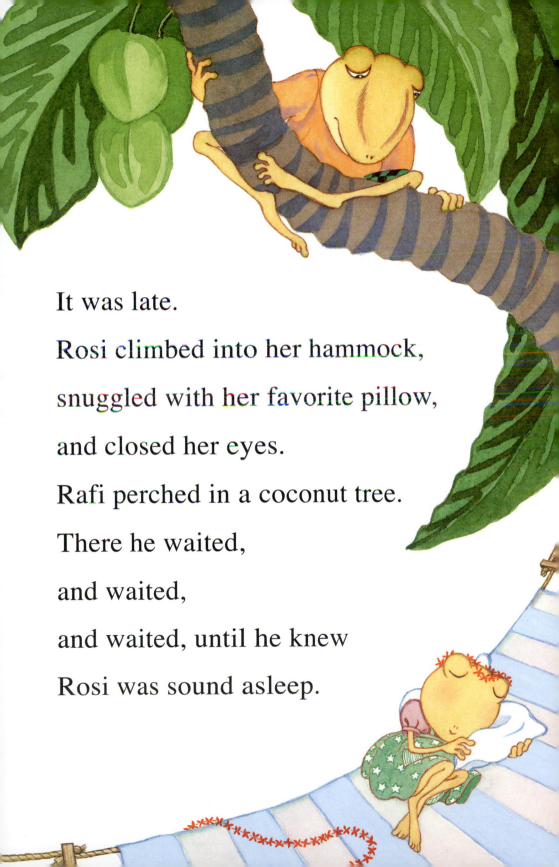

It was late.

Rosi climbed into her hammock,

snuggled with her favorite pillow,

and closed her eyes.

Rafi perched in a coconut tree.

There he waited,

and waited,

and waited, until he knew

Rosi was sound asleep.

Then Rafi climbed down the tree
and hopped to the edge of the water.
The sky was perfectly black,
with no moon in sight.
It was time.
"Rosi, Rosi, wake up!" Rafi called.
"I did it! I shot an arrow to the sky
and hundred of stars
fell into the bay. Come and see!"
"You did what?" Rosi asked.

Rafi took Rosi by the hand

and led her to the water's edge.

He stirred the inky water

with the tip of his arrow.

The water twinkled as it rippled.

"Wow!" said Rosi.

"Are those real stars?"

"Sure," Rafi said. "What else
could they be? Look—
there are no more stars in the sky."

Rosi picked up a stone

and threw it into the salty water.

The water shimmered to life

and burst into rings of stars.

"You are amazing, Rafi!" she said.

"I know," said Rafi.

Suddenly

Rafi heard a rumbling noise.

It was the sound of a motorboat.

He stepped in front of Rosi

and grabbed her by the arms.

"Let's go!" he told her.

"We need to go back to sleep."

Rosi didn't move.

"No," she said. "I want to play

with the stars."

As the boat came to a stop

Rafi and Rosi heard someone speak.

"The bay's water

contains tiny algae," a voice said.

"When disturbed,

these living things give out light

and make the water sparkle."

"Tiny algae . . ." said Rosi,

". . . that give out light?"

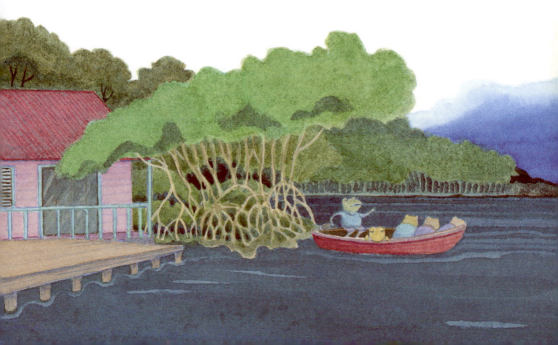

"Rafi!" Rosi screamed.

She pulled her brother

by the shirt

and with all her might

pushed him

into the inky water.

Rafi turned belly-up,

the seawater shimmering around him.

He was smiling.

"*¡Chévere!*" he called out. "It's fun!

You can make water angels."

Rosi looked at her brother.

She was dazzled by the sight.

Suddenly she wasn't mad any longer.

Maybe she could make

her own sparkling water angel

next to Rafi's.

She tested the water

with the tips of her toes, and . . .

jumped into the glittering bay.

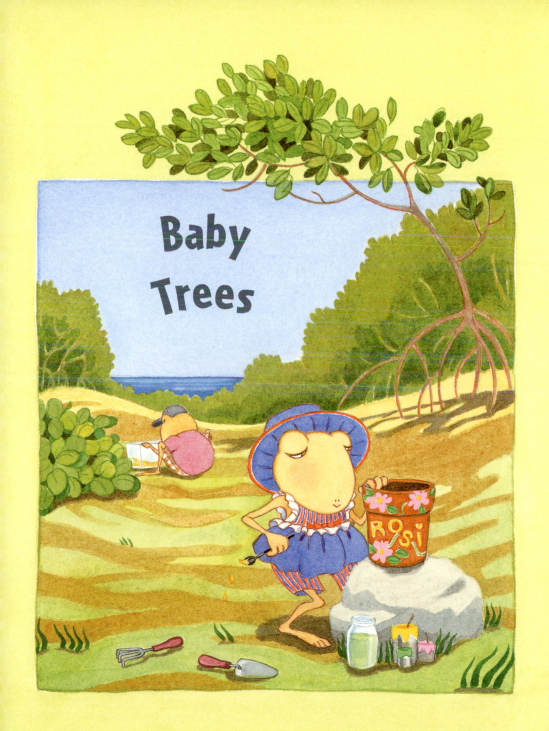

Baby Trees

Rafi had been keeping watch for days.

He knew his *cobito*

was going to change shells

any time now.

He didn't want to miss it.

"Rafi! Rafi!" Rosi called.

She found her brother staring

at the fat hermit crab

he had found among the mangroves.

"Help me get a baby tree!

I need it for my pot," said Rosi.

"*Ahorita*," said Rafi. "Later.

First, find the smallest tree

there is."

Rosi went through

the mangroves

until she found a baby tree.

She dug around it,

and pulled and tugged,

but she could not get it

out of the ground.

So she ran back to her brother.

He was sorting empty shells

inside his pet crab's tank

with a long stick.

"Rafi! Rafi!" Rosi said.

"I found the smallest tree there is.

Now, help me . . . please."

Rafi looked up at Rosi.

He looked down at her pot,

and he looked at his pet crab.

He sighed a big sigh.

"Okay, I'll help you," he said.

He placed the stick

across the corners of the tank.

"But let's hurry.
I know the *cobito*
is going to change shells
any time now."

In the mangrove forest,
Rosi led Rafi to her find.
"Here!" she said.
"That is not the smallest tree
there is!" Rafi said.
"Baby trees are always
above ground."
"How could they be?" asked Rosi.

Rafi jumped about until he found

just the mangrove he was looking for.

"Look!" he called.

Rosi looked up at a funny thing

hanging under a cluster

of yellow flowers.

"That is not a tree!" Rosi said.

"It's a seedling," said Rafi. "See?"

Rafi showed Rosi

how a red mangrove's seed

grows attached to the parent tree

until it's ready to fall off.

"I didn't know that," Rosi said.

"But I did," said Rafi with a smile.

Rafi broke off the seedling

and handed it to his sister.

"Now I need to run back to my crab

before it changes shells."

When Rafi got to the tank,

he knew something was wrong.

His crab was not inside.

Then he saw that the stick

he had been using

had fallen inside the tank,

giving the crab a way out.

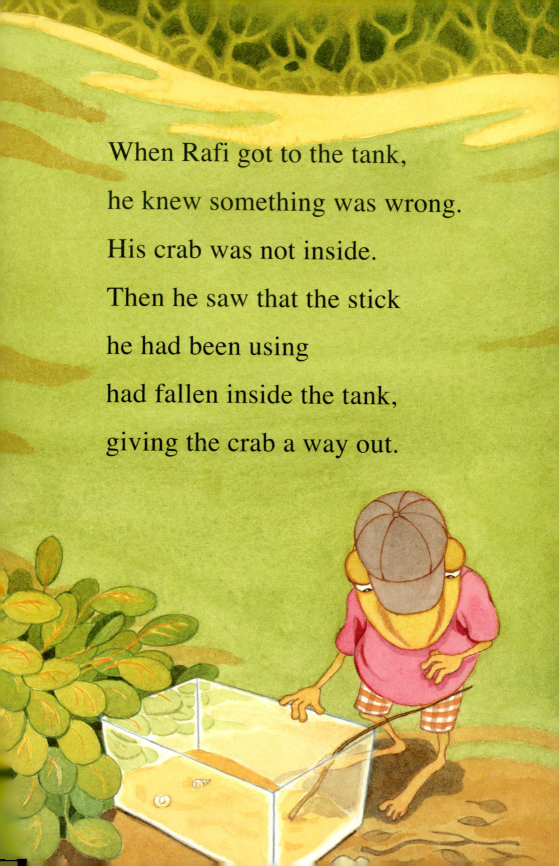

"*¡Ay, bendito!*" he yelled.

"My *cobito* escaped!"

Rafi fell to the ground.

"I had waited for so long."

He sighed.

Rosi ran over to her brother.

"I will help you," she said.

"It is useless, Rosi," said Rafi.

"My *cobito* could be anywhere."

"Just wait," Rosi told him.

"I'll try and find it."

Rosi looked all around her.

She lifted small twigs

and big leaves,

heavy stones, and light branches.

From the corners of his eyes

Rafi followed her every step.

Suddenly Rosi found some

teeny-tiny footprints.

These led her all the way

to a broken coconut.

She peeked under it.

"I think it is in here," she said.

"Really?" Rafi asked. "Let's get it!"

He jumped with his cap in one hand,

and with the other hand

he scooped up the coconut

and covered it with his cap.

"You got it!"

said Rosi.

Finally

Rafi placed the broken coconut

inside the tank.

Rafi and Rosi watched.

They watched until

very, very slowly, Rafi's *cobito*

crawled out of the coconut.

"There it is!" Rafi said.

"Look, Rosi! LOOK!"

Rafi and Rosi stared

at the hermit crab.

The *cobito* started to come out

of its snug shell.

It stopped for an instant,

and scuttled into a bigger shell,

where it got quite cozy.

The *cobito* had changed shells,

just as Rafi knew it would.

"That was SO great!" Rafi said.

Then he looked at his little sister.

"And you found it just in time."

Did You Know About . . .

. . . the Coquí?

This tiny tree frog is a beloved symbol of Puerto Rico. Found in the mountains as well as on the coast, it is usually no more than an inch and a half long. The common *coquí* can be tan, cream, gray, or even reddish brown. It often has markings over its body.

The little frog is named for its song. As soon as the sun sets on the tropical island, the males begin to serenade the females with their *CO-QUI, CO-QUI-QUI-QUI* song, until the break of dawn. The *coquí*'s song is one of the first things Puerto Ricans truly miss when they settle outside the island.

. . . Sand, Iron, and Magnets?

As you walk on the beach in Puerto Rico, you will notice the sand has gray areas. These areas contain iron deposits brought by ocean waves. Since iron is a magnetic metal, one way you can separate iron specks from the other rock particles in the sand is with a magnet.

A magnet attracts metals, like iron. When you place gray sand on a cardboard shoebox lid, and move a big magnet under it, you can draw the iron particles away from the rest of the sand.

. . . The Parguera Bioluminescent Bay?

When living things produce light they are said to be bioluminescent. The Parguera Bay, located on the southern coast of Puerto Rico, is one of just a few locations in the world where you can consistently observe bioluminescence on the surface of the water. This can best be seen on moonless nights. Movement disturbs the special kind of algae that live in the bay's water and causes the tiny living things to glow with a blue-green light. When millions of them glow together, the sea shimmers to life in a grand spectacle. It is said that bathing in the Parguera on a moonless night is like swimming among the stars.

. . . Mangroves?

A mangrove is a tropical woody tree that lives between the sea and the land in areas frequently flooded by sea tides. A community of these plants is also called a mangrove. These trees provide shelter and food for hundreds of animals, such as fish, crabs, insects, and birds.

Mangrove trees have an interesting way of reproducing. Fertilized seeds do not drop from the plants, but begin to grow spear-shaped stems and roots while still attached to the parent tree. These seedlings may grow for up to three years before breaking off from the parent tree and falling into the water in search of a place to anchor themselves.

There are several kinds of mangroves growing in the forests along the shores of Puerto Rico. The red mangrove grows closest to the sea. It stands out among others for its reddish bark and its long prop roots that give it a firm foothold against wind and waves.

. . . Hermit Crabs?

While most crabs are entirely covered in a hard armor, the hermit crab is not. The hermit crab's abdomen is very soft. In order to protect it, this crab lives in the shells once used by snails. The two pairs of legs closer to the crab's tail are much smaller than the rest, so the crab can fit snugly inside the shell. When threatened, the hermit crab withdraws deep into its shell, covering the entrance with its one big pincer.

Once the crab outgrows the shell, it uses its "feelers," or antennae, to look for a larger one. After finding the right shell, the hermit crab comes out of the old one and moves into its new home.

In Puerto Rico, hermit crabs are found along the beaches, in tidal pools, and in the mangrove forest.